# SOMETHING SWEET

## A NOVELLA

## CHRISTOPHER SWEET

*For you.*

*Bon appétit.*

# 1. Of the Carters and the Nickelsimmers

My cousin-in-law, I guess that's what you'd call my wife's cousin, used to be the so-called Ambrosia Baron. You've heard of him, or at least his legacy, if you were alive at any point this decade. It's true, I used to be related by marriage to Calvin Nickelsimmer, the very same man who brought you delicacies like Gobe Bites, Angel Nectar, and Dream Squares. If you've heard of him, which, of course you have, you know that his business exploded as a cultural phenomenon before it literally exploded in what was reported as a catastrophic accident.

It was no accident. In fact, I'm directly responsible for the demise of what he used to call his production facility and, ultimately, his livelihood. We'll get to all that. First, I need to warn you; if you've ever tried a Nickelsimmer Sweet, which you almost certainly have, you might want to sit down. Maybe take a tranquilizer, or at least have one handy.

My name is Arthur Duk and I'm a health inspector for

a modest region stretching from Taguchi, where Calvin had his so-called production facility, to New Worcestershire County. Jubilee City sits smack dab in the middle of my jurisdiction so I was also inspector for the short-lived store-front Cal eventually wound up establishing. But I'm jumping way ahead.

When I started dating Eloise Carter, she made it clear that her family is very tightly knit, which sounded great to me, being the only child of two people who were only-children themselves. The Duk clan is very small.

When we married, Eloise told me unapologetically that she would not be taking my surname, that she would sooner live as common law partners than take on the truncated name of waterfowl. My family name is a bit of an historical conundrum. The best we were ever able to figure—and by *we*, I mean my parents and I (my grandparents had all passed before I was born)—was that our name used to be Duke before an inebriated, idiotic, or possibly just apathetic ancestor of ours neglected to add the *e* at the end of our name on a significant legal document. Thus Duk and my eventual wife's early refusal to allow the name to endure on this earth. The woman ended our lineage with a swift shake of the head and a seldom-witnessed disgusted curl of the upper lip. There was very little in the way of mourning.

The first time I met Eloise's cousin Calvin was at Thanksgiving, a few months after Eloise and I were married. Her parents, Don and Audrey Carter, were hosting at their palatial farmhouse in the country. It was one of the only houses in the family that was capable of holding all of the Carters and Nickelsimmers, a truly awe-inspiring amalgamation of two huge families. Calvin and I had been to one or two of the same family events before but we had never had the occasion to actually meet. Neither of us were to blame for this; the families were so big that it took me several years to meet everyone in attendance at the many family events and, even still, I'm sure there are one or two who are still unknown to me.

Eloise's siblings alone took me a year to get to know by name. Jared, her oldest brother, was only around for the odd event. He was a documentary filmmaker and, for the first three years of mine and Eloise's relationship, he spent the bulk of his time in Iceland, where he was on the hunt for *huldufólk*, which are basically elves. When he did show up for family events, he spent a lot of time trying to convince me that he was going to catch them on film, that he'd met hundreds of witnesses who had seen *huldufólk* with their own eyes. His parents paid for the documentary and, over most of a bottle of ridiculously expensive and incredibly tasty scotch, his father confessed to me that they'd already sunk several hundred thousand dollars into the enterprise. He said this without concern. The Carters came from old money and had made that money work hard for them. None of their many children would ever want for cash.

Next came Alexandria, the Hollywood hairstylist with her own salon on Sunset Boulevard; Harrison the entrepreneur; Juliette the lawyer; Bronwyn the falconer; and Marcus, who was a poet and had legally changed his name to Maisus for reasons he couldn't ever seem to articulate. Eloise, the youngest, was a librarian and part-time horse trainer with her own little ranch attached to the Carter family farm.

Most of her siblings were married with children and both of her parents came from families as big as their own. Some holidays there were as many as eighty Carters and Nickelsimmers revelling under one roof. A motel was erected on the outskirts of town, a mile from the farm, with a business model built entirely around the frequent gatherings that took place there.

The only person who refused to attend any of the family functions was Hugo Nickelsimmer, Audrey's brother and Calvin's estranged father. According to drunken whispers that weren't so whispery as to make any attempt to avoid Calvin's ears, Hugo kept himself locked in his Victorian-style mansion in Taguchi. Whether or not his reclusiveness had anything to do with Calvin's sullenness at the gatherings, I couldn't say. It wasn't that he sulked the whole time—in fact, once I met him, he seemed quite pleasant—he was just one to keep to himself back then. He lacked the congenial, extroverted gene that everyone else in the family seemed to have inherited mountains of. It wasn't hard to see that the rest of the family didn't really know how to treat or engage with him. To me, his relative introversion was refreshing amid all the big talkers and storytellers in the family.

That Thanksgiving was, like every other Carter/Nickelsimmer holiday gathering, raucous. After dinner, Jared set up a projector and screen to show some raw footage of his hunt for Icelandic elves. The rest of the family treated the film like a rowdy burlesque show, hooting and cheering and throwing clumps of stuffing and handfuls of cranberries at the screen. Seeing them like this, it was hard to believe the majority of them were respectable, hardworking professionals out in the real world. But that's the thing about family, I guess. It allows you to behave without social limitations, relatively free of judgement. It's where we let our civic selves out for a run in the grass.

I snuck my way to the back of the room shortly after the movie started, if it could be called that—the majority of the shots seemed to be amateur B-reel footage, half of which was of bodies of water and mountains. The rest of it featured beautiful, Icelandic women, most of whom looked to be significantly younger than Jared and all of whom were indulging in some form of intoxicating substance. At first it was the girls who drew the catcalls and cheers but soon everyone was whistling at the geographical features more than the young women. It became sort of a game to keep the cheers up for the mountains or forests and then to cut them short as soon as one of the girls appeared on screen.

I chuckled from my shadowed corner when it became apparent what the game was but it soon grew to be more tiresome than entertaining, to me anyway. During a particularly rowdy reaction to a long shot of the relatively featureless base of an inactive volcano, I decided to find a quieter spot in the house to digest the ample helping of supper I'd consumed. I turned away from the screen and found myself face-to-face with Calvin Nickelsimmer, dressed in a rumpled white button-up and faded jeans, dark hair hanging limply over his eyes. He'd apparently been standing right behind me.

"Some movie, huh?" I said to him, fighting to keep all traces of irony from my voice.

He shrugged. "Iceland looks very gray."

I laughed at that, which seemed to catch him off guard. Apparently he wasn't trying to be funny.

I offered him my hand. "I'm—"

"Arthur right?" he said, giving my hand a limp shake. "Eloise's beau. I'm Calvin. I guess I'm the black sheep of the clan."

"A black sheep in a clan of chimpanzees," I said. And then, "Oh my God, I didn't mean that. I've had too much whiskey. I love this family—I don't think any of them are simian."

But Calvin was laughing. A little too hard, maybe.

"That's one of the most accurate things anyone has ever said about me. I'm a black sheep in a family of chimps," he said when he could breathe again.

We made our way to the kitchen and poured ourselves a couple of drinks. Calvin told me about himself; he was about my age—mid thirties, a bachelor, and worked as a sous chef at a place on the outskirts of Jubilee City called Yeste's.

"Pronounced like testes," he said, taking a long sip of his scotch and soda. "And don't be impressed by the job title, I'm the *only* licensed chef they have on staff and most of what we serve is simple pub food. I made them put 'sous' in my job title so it would look better on a resume when eventually I moved on to greener pastures."

I said, "I guess I'm on the dark side from where you stand. I'm a health inspector for the region. Don't recall ever visiting Yeste's but I'm sure you've met some of my colleagues."

He didn't give me the raised eyebrow most food service

professionals shoot my way when they find out what my occupation is, merely nodded at my admission.

That night, Eloise and I made love in her old room, the way only drunk, relatively newlywed couples can enjoy. We sullied every nook and cranny of that room before falling back on the bed, exhausted.

"I met your cousin Calvin tonight," I told her as I stroked her wavy, brown hair.

"Hm," she muttered. "Poor guy's always alone—he never quite fit in with the family. I'm glad you spent some time with him. He probably appreciated that. My diplomat." She gave my manhood an appreciative squeeze but it was fast asleep ahead of us and gave no indication it had felt anything.

"His folks still around?"

Eloise moved her hand up to my chest and toyed with the coils of hair that speckled it. "I barely remember them but they seemed happy. His mom, my Aunt Tina, took off when we were young. Soon after she left, his dad went into kind of a funk. He became depressed and stopped coming to family events. My mom went to check on him a couple of times. She said he wants to stay locked up in his house. Nothing anyone can do about it." She sighed.

"I got the impression from Cal that they don't really get along."

I felt Eloise shrug.

"I guess not," she said. "I'm ashamed to say it but I don't talk to Calvin much. I think they just drifted apart. Hugo became so reclusive, he cut off ties with his own son along with the rest of the family, or at least stopped making any effort to maintain their relationship."

"Maybe I should go see him sometime at work and say hi," I said. "Maybe he could use a friend."

Eloise kissed my chest. "You're sweet. But no chef wants a health inspector, family or not, visiting them at work."

I had to concur with that theory.

Two nights later, back at home, in our own bed, Eloise got a text message from Maisus saying Uncle Hugo had died. We went to the funeral a few days after that and I only barely caught a glimpse of Calvin. The poor guy seemed so alone, even surrounded by the numerous Carters and Nickelsimmers in attendance. He was wearing the same thing I'd seen him in at Thanksgiving—white shirtsleeves tucked into jeans. I shook his hand and told him to give me a shout if he needed anything. He seemed to genuinely appreciate that. His face was lined with exhaustion and grief so I didn't put much more effort into engaging him. I realized I wanted to be his friend as much I assumed he needed me to be his.

When we saw him again for Christmas, a month later, he was a different person entirely.

# 2. A Calling

If Thanksgiving at the Carter farm was like a Super Bowl party, Christmas was akin to Mardi Gras. Eloise and I arrived late in the afternoon on Christmas Eve to find that her siblings and father had already been drinking for hours. Jared, Harrison, Maisus, and Don were watching an Italian cooking show—in Italian—on the giant TV, hollering at the tops of their lungs to describe exactly what the host was doing while, in the kitchen, Alexandria attempted to recreate the dish.

"Mushrooms!" Maisus shouted as we came in and poured ourselves a couple of drinks.

"No mushrooms," Alexandria called from the kitchen. "I found a can of water chestnuts, I'll use those."

The men exploded in laughter.

They kept this up even as the house filled with extended family members. Just as I was wondering how dinner was going to be made with Alexandria, egged on by her brothers and Don, cooking what smelled like burning garden soil in the kitchen, the doorbell rang and a parade of caterers marched through the door and immediately began setting up tables with steaming dishes of hors d'oeuvres and assorted tapas that they'd been preparing in one of the outbuildings for the last several hours. Apparently Audrey Carter née Nickelsimmer had foreseen her husband's and children's shenanigans and had set the catering company up with their own space and equipment, away from the dangers of her intoxicated family.

The food was exquisite, as it always was at these events, and the drink flowed freely. It didn't take long for both Eloise and I to reach the point of Italian cooking show appreciation, but by then the game had changed to sausage roll skeet shooting, in which Harrison would toss a sausage roll and around a dozen people would try to hit it out of the air with whatever was at hand; dinner rolls, beer cans, cutlery. Nobody could ever tell if the roll was hit or with what or by whom but the game went on for half an hour or more.

It was as this newest amusement was losing the attention of its competitors that the front door opened and shut with a bang and a smartly dressed young man carrying a huge, pink box stepped into the arena-sized living room. At first I didn't recognize the newcomer; nobody seemed to. He looked over the top of his box at us as the family collectively puzzled over who this unexpected guest might be.

"Calvin?" Bronwyn said from somewhere in the room.

The man smiled and I, along with everyone else, realized it was him indeed. He'd undergone a complete transformation. Instead of the wrinkled shirt and jeans, he wore what looked like a tailored, slim-fitting, slate-gray suit. His hair looked like it had received a hundred-dollar treatment that morning. He looked younger and more vital than he had on the two previous occasions that I'd seen him. Judging by the faces of the rest of the family gathered, I wasn't the only one who'd never witnessed him looking like this.

He gave the room a confident smile and said, "Merry Christmas!"

Even his voice sounded deeper, more solid.

"It's good to see you, young man," Don bellowed, slinging an arm around Calvin's shoulders. He called into the room, "Someone get this lad a drink."

Jared was already on his way with a Manhattan while Audrey held her hands out for the box. Calvin relinquished it and accepted the drink in a fluid motion that looked choreographed. He had all the air of a celebrity politician about him.

"I guess Uncle Hugo was holding him back," Eloise murmured to me.

"What's in the box?" someone called.

Calvin addressed the room and, once more, I was reminded of a politician at work. He raised his glass and said, "Ladies and gentlemen, Carters and Nickelsimmers," he looked at me, "And Duks."

Someone quacked. The room howled with inebriated laughter and Calvin waited patiently, one hand holding his drink and the other loosely resting in a pants pocket, with a congenial smile on his lips and a twinkle in his eyes.

The room quieted on its own, quickly, like he'd cast a spell. I was captivated by him, by his seemingly natural—and sudden—ability to control a crowd without saying a word, and by what might be in the box.

"I've found my calling," he said, when he had the room's attention once more. "It's not something I would've imagined myself doing but, now that I've embraced it, I can't imagine doing anything else. You can open the box, Aunt Audrey."

She wasted no time in slipping her finger into the opening and lifting the lid. An aroma so heavenly filled the room that everyone went silent save for the occasional slurp of someone reigning in the drool pooling in their mouth. The smell was like toasted sugar and butter, with a hint of something akin to cinnamon without the spiciness. But it was also so much more than that; there was something indefinably intoxicating about that smell.

Audrey stared into the box with her mouth half open in what I was surprised to find myself imagining was the face she made when she orgasmed. I blushed with the thought and had to look away from her for fear someone would see me and be able to tell what I was thinking. When I turned to Eloise, I found that she had the exact same expression—and hers, I knew, *was* the face she made when she orgasmed. Looking around the room, I saw everyone wore a similar expression; like they were experiencing a stoned, euphoric bliss. I probably had the same look on my own face. Whatever was in the box, we all wanted it.

Calvin watched us drool for a moment then reached out and closed the lid of the box, which only partially broke the spell it had us all under.

One of the caterers, a pretty girl in chef's whites, swept through the room, clearing away dishes. She stole glances at the box every few seconds. No one could blame her; we were all under its spell. As she walked past Calvin, he grabbed her by the arm.

"Leave the dishes, take the box," he said to her. "Plate and serve, if you would. Please."

The caterer's eyes lit up. She handed the dishes off to one of her co-workers, who had just stepped into the room, and held her hands out to accept the box from Eloise's mother. Audrey looked like she would break down if she had to relinquish it. Her face took on a look of protective greed that reminded me of Gollum in the *Lord of the Rings* movies.

"It's okay, Aunt Audrey," Calvin said, placing a hand on her arm. "She'll bring them right back and you'll get to try one. Two, if you're lucky."

Audrey surrendered the box with a groan. The rest of us let out a commiserative sigh, as if we all experienced parting grief along with her.

The caterer turned to leave with the box and Calvin grabbed her by the arm again, a bit harder this time, I thought. If he hurt her, though, she gave no indication.

"These are for party guests only," he said. "I know how many are there. Do not touch them with your hands, use tongs."

He released her arm and she hurried into the kitchen, bearing the box like a priestess with a sacred relic.

A tense silence filled the room while we waited for her to return with Calvin's mystery treats. People shuffled around distractedly, taking tiny sips from their drinks, afraid of dispelling the memory of the aroma by ingesting anything else. Calvin, all the while, smiled at his family in contented silence. I wanted to talk to him but all I could think about was tasting whatever was in that box.

After what felt like far too long of a wait, the caterer appeared in the door to the living room, followed by five of her colleagues. Each of them carried an enormous serving platter full of dessert plates, atop which were something that looked like donuts from where I stood, across the room. Each of the servers wore an expression of frustrated grief. One of them, a thin guy in his twenties, looked like he'd been crying.

The bewitching aroma of the desserts spread throughout the room and we were all stoned once more by how good they smelled.

"These," Calvin said, "I call Gobe Bites."

I lost all sense of the rest of the room when I received mine, so I can't really say what anyone else's reaction was. When I spoke to Eloise about it later, she said it was as thought she'd left her body and ascended to a higher plane as soon as the dessert touched her lips. It was the perfect way to describe it. Ascension.

Gobe Bite was something of a misnomer—each pastry was the size of a large dinner bun and took up most of a dessert saucer. The "Gobe" part of it, I later learned, was arbitrarily assigned to the treat for no other reason than that it sounded good. The bulk of the thing was an orangey-brown that glistened with a sweet glaze that, incredibly, was not sticky in the slightest; it was more like a thick oil. It was topped with a cream-colored icing, which itself was bisected by an almost effervescent purple squiggle of some kind of jelly. When I picked it up, it was much lighter than I had expected it to be. It was soft but firm, the consistency of a hardboiled egg.

Biting into it was one of the single most pleasurable moments of my life. I felt guilty about how much I enjoyed it but my unease was quickly assuaged by the sheer bliss I experienced, as well as the knowledge that everyone else was feeling something similar.

The orange outer layer gave way to a cakey inside that was the same nearly-glowing purple color as the squiggle of jelly on top. The textures melted together in my mouth, coming alive in an almost literal sense; like a small, slippery creature was pleasuring me from within my mouth—rolling over my tongue and caressing the insides of my cheeks, teasing my gums, and stroking each of my teeth. Swallowing it was an absurdly sexual experience.

The next five minutes sounded like the world's biggest orgy. Moans of pleasure and gasps of ecstasy mingled with grunts of primal satisfaction. The sounds of chewing and the smacking of lips added to the coital soundtrack, which went perfectly with what I felt as I consumed the Gobe Bite. Time seemed to stretch as I consumed it, though, when I finished, it all felt like it had happened too fast.

When the last bite had been swallowed—nobody savored theirs—the room once more fell silent. We regarded each other with the bashful awkwardness of new lovers. We may as well have actually had a giant orgy.

After a long silence, Jared said, "That was transcendent."

The rest of us gushed our agreement and gradually ramped back up to the drunken reveling we'd been in the midst of before Calvin had shown up with his pink box of magical treats.

Calvin was the star of the show for the rest of the night. He effortlessly worked the room, greeting family with warm hugs and handshakes, as if he hadn't been the awkward guy standing in the corner at every gathering up until now.

I suppose I felt a modicum of bitterness toward him that night when I couldn't manage to get his attention for more than a quick handshake. I'd been the only one who was able to connect with him a month ago and had assumed we might become something like friends. I liked the quiet, reserved Calvin. That's not to say I didn't enjoy this new version of him, it just seemed like now there was a protective veneer to get past. I decided I'd catch up with him after the holidays, when he was no longer the new family favorite.

Much later that night, in her old bedroom once again, Eloise closed the door behind us and went straight to her closet. When she opened the door, the aroma told me exactly what she'd hidden in there. My blood started flowing south the moment I smelled it.

She put the Gobe Bite in her mouth and unclasped her dress with one hand, letting it fall to the floor around her. She wore nothing underneath. I barely managed to wriggle out of my clothes by the time she got to the bed, which was good because she practically fell on top of me, pressing her mouth to mine with the Gobe Bite still in it. We made fast, rough love with the dessert between us, gnashing and licking at it like a couple of dogs as we screwed.

There wasn't a crumb left by the time we finished.

# 3. Nickelsimmer Sweets

A couple of months went by and I'd all but forgotten about Calvin and his newfound passion. If I had given it any thought at all, I likely would have assumed that it was a phase he'd been going through—a way of dealing with his dad's death, one that his entire family reaped the benefit of for one magical Christmas night. The memory of the Gobe Bites seemed like an exaggerated one. No way something could be *that* good. More likely we were all simply drunk enough to enjoy an exceptionally delicious pastry in primal fashion. I barely even thought about them when I got the work order for an inspection at Yeste's, where Calvin worked.

I called ahead as soon as I saw the job pop up on my laptop screen but nobody answered. It was around noon so the safe assumption was that the restaurant was busy with their lunch rush.

I didn't normally make a practice of calling ahead to establishments I was due to inspect, that was sort of antithetical to the whole surprise inspection part of my job. If restaurants knew we were coming, they'd have enough time to hide or disguise any number of major infractions, not that I expected any from Yeste's. In general, any place that's been open for more than a couple of years isn't going to get dinged for anything major; experienced restaurant owners know how to comply with health regulations, even if it's just enough to get by. I'd called to give Calvin a heads up because I hadn't spoken to him since Christmas and would have felt like a world-class douche if the first time we'd seen each other in months was so that I could critique the cleanliness of his work environment. I've yet to meet a chef who doesn't take health inspections personally.

As it turned out, I didn't have to worry about offending Calvin because he wasn't there when I showed up. In fact, as I was told by the general manager, Calvin had resigned just after New Year's. I asked about where he was working now and the GM, who dressed like every GM—shirtsleeves that barely contained a protruding gut, tucked into tan, off-brand chinos—raised his eyebrows at me like I'd just told him I parked my tyrannosaurus out back and could he please have someone go out to brush its teeth.

"He's your family," the GM said with unmasked incredulity. "How could you not know about Nickel-simmer Sweets?"

I merely shook my head.

The GM scratched something out on the back of one of his business cards and handed it to me. "His storefront opens next month."

He'd scribbled down an address in Jubilee City, on Opal Street of all places, the most affluent street in the city with no fewer than half a dozen Starbucks spread along the three miles it ran before terminating at a park on one end and turning into an industrial road at the other.

"This is where his shop is?" I asked, recalling those extraordinary desserts he'd brought to Christmas.

The GM nodded. "That's where his *first* shop is. If he doesn't have two more open by next spring, the boy's an imbecile. Tell him Gerard says hello when you see him."

I told Gerard the GM I'd do just that and then handed him my list of recommendations to avoid closure.

By the time I got into the city, I was fighting through evening rush hour traffic and didn't make it to Calvin's store until close to supper. I'd called Eloise on the road and told her not to expect me. I asked her if she'd heard of Nickelsimmer Sweets but she claimed ignorance of any new venture of her cousin's.

"I haven't heard from him since Christmas, when he brought those...things," she said, unable to control the desire in her voice when she alluded to the Gobe Bites.

My pants grew tighter at her mention of them. I'd been passing the damn things off as some shared drunken mania but from the moment Gerard mentioned Nickelsimmer Sweets, the memory of the Gobe Bites had been flitting through my consciousness. Hearing the naked lust in my wife's voice amplified my own desire for them.

I promised Eloise I'd update her with what I found out as soon as I'd spoken to Calvin. She told me to invite him to the house for dinner sometime in the next week and I couldn't help but wonder if her motivation lay in the hope that he would bring more of his aphrodisiacal desserts.

The good thing about showing up after five was that it

was relatively easy to find parking that wouldn't cost me half of my earnings. While I was tempted to expense the parking, I didn't want to have to face any questions about my cousin-in-law's new business if one of my superiors decided to investigate my unplanned trip to Jubilee City.

When I arrived at the address Gerard had given me, I was disheartened to see the windows and door were papered over. Taped to the inside of the window was a handwritten note that said: COMING SOON! NICKELSIMMER SWEETS!

I searched for an opening in the paper covering the windows that I might be able to peek through, but Calvin had done a thorough job of concealing the interior from any lookie-loos. I cursed and turned away from the shopfront, scanning the lively street for somewhere to grab a quick dinner. The street was bustling with after-work traffic; mainly pedestrians strutting to their favorite happy hour spot and couples in cars scoping out somewhere to eat.

"Arthur?"

The voice came from behind me and right away I knew Calvin's newfound confidence hadn't been a mere flash in the pan. He was just locking the front door of the shop behind him when I turned around and I internally scolded myself for missing my opportunity to see inside. He looked the part of the owner of a new Opal Street business, in designer jeans and a tucked in polo shirt with a leather messenger bag slung over one shoulder.

We shook hands—his grip was strong and firm—and I explained that his old manager had told me about his new venture.

"Never should have given that idiot the address,"

Calvin muttered as he led me away from the shop. "He needed somewhere to send my parting paperwork and for some reason I told him to send it here. Oh well. Glad you came by. Let's grab some dinner."

"I was hoping to see your new shop, if you'd let me," I told him, only slightly resisting him guiding me away from the place.

He clucked his tongue at me. "No peeking yet. I planned on telling the family about it when I sent out my grand opening invitations." His voice took on a serious edge. "Promise you'll keep it to yourself."

"Yeah, of course," I said. "I mean, I told Eloise I was coming to see your new shop but she'll keep it quiet."

Calvin swore. "She's probably already called her brothers and sisters to find out if they know anything."

He wasn't wrong and I didn't insult him by disagreeing or trying to defend her. In truth, Eloise couldn't keep a secret to save her life.

We found a quiet pub around the corner and ordered a pitcher and a couple of burgers. Calvin evaded every question I posed to him about Nickelsimmer Sweets. Most were met with a smug grin and a shake of the head. Then I asked the right question, or the wrong one, depending on how you look at it. It was the question that sealed the fates of both Calvin and his new business, though neither of us could have known it. Or maybe Calvin did know. Maybe he wanted me to learn the secrets of Nickelsimmer Sweets and bring about the eventual ruin of one of the most widespread and short-lived culinary phenomenons in history.

"What about your initial health inspection?" I inquired

as casually as possible. "You need it to open the store. I could pull some strings and do the inspection for you."

This was a big no-no. You don't inspect the business of family and friends if you can help it. If a serious infraction was found, it was either report the friend or family member and potentially kill their business, or don't report it and risk being charged with fraud. None of these thoughts even crossed my mind as I watched him turn the question over. Besides, a new opening has very little to worry about from us, everything in there would be new and shiny and the only thing I'd really have to look for was hand-washing sinks in the right places, proper ventilation, and a plan for pest control that didn't include a cat.

He took a long sip of his beer and said, "That's a good idea. Saves me from having to keep everything secret from one more person. I can trust you to keep your mouth shut, right?"

"Sure." I was willing to agree to almost any terms to catch a glimpse, and hopefully a sample, of what he was working on.

We agreed to meet at his shop the following week. I knew I would have no trouble having myself assigned to it. When the initial inspection was done, I could hand the reigns over to one of my colleagues to avoid any further conflict of interest.

"Almost forgot," Calvin said before we parted ways. He rooted around in his bag and procured an ivory-colored envelope, which he held out to me with both hands, like an offering. "It's yours and Eloise's invitation to my grand opening in a couple of weeks. I was going to drop them in the mail on the way home."

"We'll be there," I promised. "See you next week."

We shook hands once more, like old business partners more than family, and went out separate ways.

It was well past dark when I got home that night. I came into the house to find Eloise sprawled out on the couch, watching an old episode of *Cake Boss* with one hand holding a glass of chardonnay and the other elbow-deep in a giant bag of cheese-flavored popcorn. It was a combination that sickened me to think about, but always brought a smile to my face when I saw my otherwise dainty wife indulging in it.

I gave her a peck on the forehead and dropped the invitation on the coffee table in front of her. She eyeballed it without removing her hand from the popcorn bag or putting the wine glass down.

"An invitation," I said in response to her raised eyebrows. "To Calvin's grand opening. I'm going to have a shower."

I had just toweled off and was grabbing a fresh pair of jockeys from my dresser when I heard the bedroom door open behind me. The smell struck me a second after and my entire body reacted. My skin, already warm from the shower, heated up and prickled with beads of sweat. My neck tingled, my stomach fluttered, and my organ became painfully stiff. I turned to see Eloise standing in the door, holding the open invitation envelope in her hand. The aroma was coming from the card and, while it wasn't the exact same smell the Gobe Bites gave off, it was clearly in the same genus. It had similar buttery undertones but came with a fruitier, livelier smell. The look in Eloise's eyes told me exactly what she wanted, which was exactly what I wanted. I didn't even ask what was on the invitation until after we'd both exorcised our carnal desires.

As we lay side-by-side, naked and panting in post-coital exhaustion, Eloise slapped the invitation onto my chest.

"There will be samples," she said.

I had a moment of anxiety when I considered what would happen when a bunch of strangers caught that aroma, never mind actually consuming the sweets. I imagined a rave, but instead of glow-sticks, people held pastries in each hand.

It had occurred to me, soon after Christmas, that Calvin may have drugged the desserts, but that wouldn't explain their intoxicating aroma. Would it? I dismissed the notion soon after thinking it up, but I—like thousands or tens of thousands more in the very near future—would often lay awake at night wondering how he managed to create such galvanizing desserts. And I eventually got to find out. Lucky me.

The invitation was on heavy, expensive paper, the front of which bore a more whimsical logo than I would have imagined; *Nickelsimmer Sweets* in cotton candy pink, with the bottom of the last *s* encircling the words and terminating in a curly-q. The message inside, in the same enticing pink, read: *You are most cordially invited to the Grand Opening of Nickelsimmer Sweets! Date: April 12. Place: 2911 Opal Street, Jubilee City. Save room for samples!*

"I take it you'll be joining me," I said, handing the invitation back to her after first taking a long sniff of the inside and shuddering in olfactory pleasure.

Eloise smirked at me. "I'd consider it cheating if you went alone."

She pulled me on top of her and we made love again, slowly this time.

# 4. The Inspection

The week leading up to my inspection of Nickelsimmer Sweets dragged by. I felt like a kid waiting for Christmas to arrive. It troubled me a bit that I was so infatuated with Calvin's fancy desserts, but their allure couldn't be ignored.

We kept the invitation by our bed but its aroma faded pretty quickly—I know because the next morning I shoved my nose in it and inhaled deeply, smelling only paper and dried ink. It was probably for the better; who knows if either of us would have been able to keep our hands off it if the paper had retained its captivating scent.

I didn't hear from Calvin for the week leading up to my visit and resisted every urge to check in to see how things were going. If he needed or wanted help or someone to talk to about his new business, he knew how to get a hold of me. I caught myself typing out a text message to him on more than one occasion, reaching at excuses to speak with him. Eloise had indeed called her siblings to dig for information on Calvin, which, along with the invitations to the grand opening that followed shortly after, likely meant that he was being harassed by everyone else in the family. I felt smug self-satisfaction at the fact that I would get to see the shop before any of the Carters or Nickelsimmers, and held onto my pride in that privilege to keep myself from going stir crazy while I waited for the day of the inspection to arrive.

When the day finally came, I could hardly contain myself. Even Eloise was jittery with sympathetic anticipation. For some reason, I had expected her to be resentful that I was getting an early look at the business but I suspect I was projecting my own emotional persona onto her—*I* was the one who was broody and sensitive, while she was more like an emotional butterfly, constantly aflutter, capable of tumbling out of the way of danger in a way that seemed almost accidental at times.

I got up before the sun that morning, though I wasn't due to meet with Calvin at his shop until two o'clock. Even allowing plenty of time for the drive, I had nothing to do with myself for the hours between waking and my impending appointment. When Eloise came downstairs, two hours after I'd risen, I had high hopes of an early morning roll in the hay with her to keep my mind off the inspection (or perhaps because I *couldn't* keep my mind off it) but she was due at the library first thing for a conference. She dodged my eager pinches and grabs while she poured herself coffee and grabbed a piece of toast and an apple on her way out.

"Call me as soon as you're done," she said, planting a light peck on my cheek and heading for the door. "I want to hear all about what Cal's been up to over there. I still can not believe he got a storefront on Opal."

"The second I get back in the car," I promised. Then, "You sure I can't tempt you to be late for your meeting?"

She punched me on the shoulder then slid her hand down to my groin and squeezed what she found waiting for her. She gave me a devilish grin and said, "You can take care of yourself. I have to go."

Her car was barely out of the driveway before I was getting down to business with myself in the same spot she'd been lounging on the couch the night before.

The rest of the morning dragged. I tried to distract myself with some work I had outstanding but couldn't keep my mind on it. Instead, I found myself thinking about the Gobe Bites we'd had at the Carter farm. I mulled over what they may be made from, not that I knew the first thing about baking or what went into which dessert. I reflected on the texture; like firm gelato in parts and hardboiled eggs in others, though even those comparisons fell far from the mark. Still, they were the only comparison I could come up with. Eggs or an incredibly tender meat, like scallops.

Once the thought was there, I realized that was exactly what the dessert had felt like in my mouth—a little bit firmer and it would have come across as rubbery. I pondered how delicate a process it must be for Calvin to get them to be the exact consistency they were.

That thinking led me down a rabbit hole of day dreams about what other kinds of treats he had in store for the grand opening. What new concoctions might he come up with in the days, weeks, and years ahead? And how much money would we and the rest of the world wind up sinking into it? How much of our personal savings would Eloise and I end up blowing on Nickelsimmer Sweets?

For the first time, I realized Calvin was on the verge of becoming very rich, very quickly if he played his cards right.

After parking in the same lot as the week before, which cost ten dollars more during business hours, I all but ran to 2911 Opal Street and was delighted to see that the signage had been installed over the door. Loud, pink letters spelled out NICKELSIMMER SWEETS over the awning. The same thing—in the same style as the invitations, with the last *s* swooping around the words—was painted over the big display window, which was still papered over.

I rapped on the glass of the front door and surveyed the street around me. It was unseasonably warm and many of the cafes and restaurants had put out their patio furniture. Millennials sipped craft beer and munched on avocado toast, oblivious to the life-changing confection that would soon be loosed upon the street and the world.

"Ready?"

I was startled for the second time by Calvin coming out of his shop without me noticing. This time, though, he was holding the door open for me.

"You know you're going to be the hottest thing on this street, right?" I said. "I hope you've hired help."

Calvin only smiled and motioned me into the shop with a nod of his head.

I don't know what possessed me to think I would be walking into a lively funhouse like one of the lucky brats who'd won Wonka's golden ticket, but I found it hard to conceal my disappointment when I stepped inside to find the place empty save for half a dozen bistro tables, their chairs stacked and still wrapped in cellophane, an empty display case, and similarly empty shelves behind the counter. Instead of the bewitching aroma of Calvin's desserts, I was treated to the sterile smell of newly installed food preparation equipment. It was no different than the dozens of other inspections I'd performed at restaurants and bakeries that had yet to open. Why had I assumed this would be different?

"Sorry, pal," Calvin said, leading me toward the cash counter. "I know you were hoping for a sample but I need to pass my inspection before I can commence production."

He was right but I couldn't help feeling agitated, like he'd somehow led me on. The look in his eyes told me he'd known exactly what I'd been after and how disappointed I'd be when I didn't get it.

I raised my hand in what I hoped looked like a solemn gesture. "It's against the rules anyway. Not supposed to accept gifts, bribes, or samples from anyone I'm inspecting." It was the truth but we both knew I was saying it to make myself feel better.

The inspection went swiftly and smoothly. Everything was in order and up to the standards set forth by those who thought they knew how people should run their business. After inspecting the front—fridges at the right temperature, hand-washing sink in place—we moved to the back of house, which was set up similar to most bakeries I'd been in, with one exception.

"Where's all of your equipment?" I asked as we walked

past an empty, stainless steel prep table. "I don't even see an oven."

Calvin shrugged. "I've got everything I need."

No baker am I but I was sure he would need something to actually bake his desserts in. Absent were the typical industrial mixer, utensils of any sort, or the giant plexiglass bins for flour and whatever other ingredients bakers used. Wire shelves and stainless steel tables and counters made up the strong majority of the room's contents. It made me a bit uncomfortable.

"You know there has to be a follow up inspection, right?" I said in as innocent a tone as I could muster. "During operating hours. Another inspector will have to be here to ensure everything's being used appropriately, ingredients stored properly, all stuff I'm sure you know about."

"Any chance you can get the assignment?" he asked without hesitation.

I said, "Listen, Calvin, if there's anything untoward going on here, I can't cover it up for you. The higher-ups will be more critical if they find out we're family."

"Who's going to know we're family? You're a Duk."

I didn't acknowledge the quip, whether intended or not. When your name also happens to be a commonly used word or the name of an animal or object, you become immune to it being taken in vain by the time you hit your twenties; much sooner if you're not the sensitive type, which I am.

"With all the social media outlets these days, anyone could stumble across our relationship completely acciden-tally, never mind if they were looking for anything, which my bosses will be when I uncharacteristically request being assigned for the follow up visit," I said.

Calvin screwed up his face. "Relationship? Don't make things weird."

"Family relationship."

"Either way," he said, "There's nothing like that to worry about. I've got a good thing going here, or I will when I open next week. If you haven't been able to tell, I'm pretty secretive about all of this. Last thing I need is some inspector thinking he can cash in by selling my trade secrets to the highest bidder."

I nodded in understanding. "Or going into their own Gobe Bite business."

"Impossible," he said without a trace of sarcasm. "Can you do it?"

"I'll see what I can make happen," I said. "Maybe I can convince my manager I just really want an excuse to get out to the city."

He clapped me on the back. "Atta boy!"

I finished up the paperwork, emailed Calvin his copy of the temporary certificate, and left him with a promise to see him the following week for the grand opening.

I called Eloise as soon as I got back in the car, as I'd told her I would.

"That is weird," she agreed once I'd told her about the inspection and the odd lack of equipment. "I'm sure he'll bring in all his utensils and bins before opening. He has to use *something* to make them, right? And some desserts are chilled instead of baked."

"I get that," I said, trying not to curse as I navigated

through the city traffic. "He just seemed a bit cagey about the whole thing."

"He must be nervous," Eloise said. "I can't imagine opening my own business; it's a huge amount of work and stress. He doesn't have any guarantee that he'll succeed."

I scoffed at that. "You and I have both tried his stuff. Just the smell of the invitation turned us into a couple of animals."

"Arthur!"

"It did, didn't it?"

"You're making me blush at work."

"Kind of wishing you'd taken me up on that morning sexy time, now aren't you?" I teased.

"Stop it, mister," she said, laughing.

We chatted about what to have for supper and I said I'd stop for some groceries since one of my favorite stores happened to be on the way home.

"Get something for dessert," she said, mischief in her voice. "Something fun."

Now it was my turn to redden. I promised I'd make it good and we said our goodbyes.

An hour-and-a-half later, I packed up my car with groceries —for dessert, I'd picked up a creme pie and had purchased an extra can of whipped cream to go with it—which took up too little trunk space considering what I'd paid. I recalled why I seldom visited my favorite grocery store; the quality of food was inarguable but the damage it did to my wallet was catastrophic.

Maybe things would have turned out differently if I hadn't indulged in fancy groceries, or maybe I would have grown suspicious enough of Calvin later on that I would have eventually done the same thing anyway. I only knew it was a hell of a coincidence, too much to pass up on, when I pulled back onto the highway right behind Calvin's new car. I hadn't seen it in person until then but he'd shown me some pictures the week prior, when we'd gone out for beers.

It was a silver Mercedes, nearly indistinguishable from the thousands of others like it that were cruising the streets, set apart only by the vanity plate Calvin had purchased for it; he'd had it framed in a cover the same pink as the writing on his shop window. The plate itself said: SW33TBYT. I'd commented how on the nose it was and Calvin had only grinned. He said he was looking into having the car vinyl-wrapped in pink with the logo on the sides, hood, and rear window.

I'm not sure I'll ever be able to decide what compelled me to tail him, beyond a burning curiosity to see what the inscrutable Calvin Nickelsimmer got up to in his life. I'm not sure I would have followed him if it hadn't been for his desserts. Since we'd tried them at Christmas, Calvin seemed to generate an irresistible gravity of his own. He himself remained a relatively uninteresting guy, but whenever I thought of his desserts, I naturally thought of him as well. I was certain others felt the same way. Certainly Eloise's eyes lit up anytime her cousin came up in conversation these days.

I knew I was committed as soon as we passed the exit I took to get home. I considered calling Eloise to tell her I'd be late but decided I'd rather not have to explain myself yet. Besides, if he didn't get off the highway soon, I would turn around and come home with my curiosity unsatisfied. I was getting hungry.

It shocked me so much when he turned onto the second exit after the one I usually took to get home, that I almost missed following him off the highway. I assumed he must be making a pit stop—I had no idea where he lived but surely if he was this close to us, we'd have seen more of him.

When he pulled into the long driveway of a massive, old Victorian ten minutes later, my jaw almost hit my knees. I recognized the house from pictures Eloise had shown me; it had once belonged to her late Uncle Hugo, Calvin's dad.

I kept driving past the house, which was the only one on the short, pot-holed road, the way I'd seen detectives do in movies when they're tailing the bad guys to their secret hideout. The road terminated in a cul-de-sac not more than thirty feet from the driveway and by the time I'd turned around and started creeping back in the direction of the house, Calvin was standing at his car door with his arms crossed, staring my way. I gave him a stupid wave and turned into the driveway. He marched down the lane to meet me as I got out of my car.

"What are you doing here?" he snapped.

I offered him my best conciliatory grin. "Saw you on the highway as I was heading home and couldn't resist. Figured I'd see where you've been hanging your hat these days. Got a cold beer inside?"

"No beer, sorry," he said, not sounding sorry at all.

"All good. Want to show me around?"

"Not particularly."

The tension was so unexpected that my brain just couldn't grasp what he was saying to me. I chuckled and started to walk past him.

"Can I just use the bathroom then? Should've gone before I left your shop."

He grabbed my arm a lot harder than was necessary and pulled me back toward my car.

"I appreciate that you want to snoop—"

"Nothing like that," I interrupted.

He held up a hand. "Whatever your intention was when you followed me home, I need you to go. Now."

I said, "Did I do something to piss you off, Cal?"

"You followed me home. Next time, call. I'll see you at the grand opening."

He practically shoved me back into my car and almost chopped my foot off closing the door behind me. He stood watching me with his hands in his pockets as I reversed out of the driveway and headed back toward home.

# 5. Suspicions

"I can't believe you followed him home, Arthur."

I had expected Eloise to take my side in the matter and was as unprepared for her outrage as I had been for Calvin's.

"You don't think it's weird that he doesn't want anyone knowing he's living at his dad's old place?"

"It's none of our business!"

We hadn't had a fight like this in a long time. Our creme pie sat forgotten on the kitchen counter, losing more pizazz with every minute it remained unrefrigerated.

"Actually," I said, slipping into health inspector mode, "If I suspect there's something fishy about the way he's running his business, I have an obligation to look into the matter."

Eloise coughed out something that might have been a laugh. "You're a health inspector, not a cop. You don't get to tail people like some gumshoe. Where he lives has nothing to do with the food he serves. And didn't you say he passed his inspection?"

"Provisionally."

She left the room then. I called after her but the only response I received was the percussion of her angry footsteps up the stairs, followed by the slamming of our bedroom door.

I cooked our supper, ribeye steaks with asparagus and baby red potatoes, and set the table for two. Eloise's food sat untouched even as I cleared away my own dishes and guzzled a third glass of red. I covered her plate and put it in the fridge. The deflated pie went in the trash.

Eloise didn't make an appearance for the rest of the evening, though I could hear her moving around upstairs, going through her nightly ritual as if nothing was amiss. I drank more wine and passed out on the couch.

That night, I dreamed that I followed Calvin home once more. In my dream, his car was hot pink and had Gobe Bites stuck all over it, the way people sometimes decorate a newlywed couple's limousine with blossoms. His dad's old house glowered down at me as I pulled into the driveway, the sky behind it glowed the same burnt orange as the Gobe Bites. Even though I hadn't seen him go into the house, Calvin's car was empty when I approached it. I inched up the creaking wooden steps to the door and let myself in. The inside of the house was the back room of Nickelsimmer Sweets, except now it was bustling with activity. Faceless figures in kitchen whites worked soundlessly—kneading dough, portioning out ingredients, and glazing pastries that resembled glistening hornet's nests. On a long, stainless-steel prep table, Calvin lay on his back, naked. Straddling him, also naked, was Eloise, hips moving in liquid rhythm, her head thrown back in ecstasy. My wife saw me and smiled. She held out her hand to me, beckoning. Calvin spotted me and outstretched his own hand, which held a beating heart, decorated with piping of bright green icing. Eloise grabbed the hand holding the heart and brought it to her mouth. She bit into the heart and her movement on top of Calvin intensified. She screamed but it was one of primal fury more than sexual bliss. Calvin lay back and took a bite as well. Blood mixed with the brilliant green icing and dripped down his chin. Eloise climbed off of him but their skin remained joined together, stretching between them like taffy as she moved away from him, sauntering towards me in a strut I would have found appealing in other circumstances. Their shared flesh stretched taught and, as she got closer to me, I could make out small, black orbs passing through the skin between them, moving from Calvin's groin to her own. The orbs flowed into her and contorted her flesh as they slid underneath it to various parts of her body; her legs, then her stomach, her hands, and finally her head. The biggest orb of all, the size of a basketball, came out of Calvin last. It was so heavy that it made the skin between them sag and hit the floor. When it passed into Eloise, it moved into her stomach, distending it as though she were nine months pregnant. The huge orb slid upwards, past her bare breasts, jostling them as it went, and up her throat. As it reached the top of her neck, her head slid off as though it had never really been attached. A Gobe Bite squeezed through the hole and took her head's place. Calvin started clapping and the faceless bakers joined in, their applause a cacophonous staccato that turned into a sound like white noise.

I woke up to blessed silence, soaked in sweat on the

living room floor, apparently having thrashed myself off the couch in my sleep.

The rest of the week leading up to the grand opening was tense between Eloise and I. The closer we got to the date, the more agitated we seemed to grow with one another. We fought about things that had never been an issue before; a single wine glass left on the counter, a door closed too hard, parking too close to the garage. I continued to sleep on the couch.

Three days after the fight that started it all, I went out for lunch with her brother Jared, who was in town for the grand opening. We met at a bistro we both liked. I ordered a reuben sandwich with the soup of the day. Jared got the keto bowl. The second the waiter left with our orders, I grilled Jared about his late Uncle Hugo.

"He was a weird cat," Jared said, sipping the IPA he'd ordered to go with his meal. "Stopped coming to family events a while back. My dad said he spent most of his time at home. He used to live in this creepy old house, like something out of a Tim Burton movie.

I mentioned that Calvin was living there now and recounted the little run-in we'd had.

Jared's eyebrows shot up. "No shit. He actually moved into that place? Kind of makes sense, I guess, but..." he drifted off.

"What makes sense?" I said.

"My dad said Hugo used to be a pretty normal guy; quiet but decent. Like Calvin used to be—reserved, I mean. After Aunt Tina took off, Hugo moved himself into that spooky house. Apparently they'd bought it together as a restoration project but Hugo never got around to actually doing anything with it. Calvin was away at school at the time and Hugo didn't even tell him what he was doing; didn't even tell him Tina had taken off, from what I hear. My folks went to check on him a few times but anytime someone tried to visit him there, he'd chase them off."

"Like Calvin did to me," I said.

The food came then and we spent a few minutes digging into our lunch. The reuben was perfect; buttery on the outside, hot, sweet, and tangy within.

"Do you think he's hiding something in there?" I asked as I picked a piece of sauerkraut from between my teeth.

Jared speared half a hardboiled egg with his fork and shoved it in his mouth. He chewed thoughtfully for a few seconds and said, "That's what my dad was thinking when Hugo wouldn't let anyone come around. But nobody could figure out what he might be keeping from us. Or why."

I really didn't want to share my theory with Jared but I had to bounce it off someone and Eloise certainly wouldn't hear it. Any conversation involving Calvin was a surefire way to an explosive argument. With that nightmare still fresh in my mind, I had become extra sensitive about her taking her cousin's side.

I said, "I think it's got something to do with his new business. With those desserts." I told Jared about the empty back room at Nickelsimmer Sweets.

Jared shrugged. "Seems like a stretch to me. You think his dad had a secret dessert lab and Calvin stumbled across it? Now he's making money off his daddy's research?"

"Something like that, I guess."

"Even if he did, so what?"

It was impossible to define the unease I had about the

whole thing. And I could tell Jared wasn't happy that I was on the verge of casting dispersions about the tantalizing desserts Calvin created.

"Maybe I just take my job too seriously," I said, only partly meaning it.

That seemed to set Jared at ease. He laughed and agreed then flagged our waiter down and ordered us another round of drinks. At first I demurred but Jared could be pretty convincing and next thing I knew, we were clinking our glasses and enjoying our second drink of the afternoon.

The second drink swiftly turned into a third and I decided to clear my schedule for the rest of the day. We drank until supper time then caught a cab to a steakhouse where we ate and drank like fat kings.

By the time I stumbled through the door of mine and Eloise's house that evening, it was after ten. I waved through the door to Jared, who sat in the back of the Lyft we'd shared. The Corolla, driven by a chatty guy named Dan, reversed out of the driveway and disappeared into the night.

I called into the house that I was home but got no response. Figuring Eloise was in bed already, I kicked off my shoes, poured myself a big glass of water, and flopped onto the couch.

I spent half an hour surfing through Netflix, not really paying attention to the rectangles of digital movie posters sliding by on the screen. When the front door opened, I jumped so violently the remote flew from my hand and hit the ceiling, knocking off bits of stucco that rained down on me like heavy snow.

Eloise froze when she passed the living room and saw

me sitting there. She wore the same blouse and knee-length skirt I'd seen her leave the house in that morning. Her hair was a mess.

I only stared at her, trying not to let my imagination fill in the blanks of her day for me.

"What?" she finally asked.

"Long day?" I said, looking back to the screen, absently flicking through the movie menu.

"I had to go take care of the horses," she said. "Paula was sick and couldn't make it over."

"You lost a button," I said.

The middle of her blouse was spread open in a diamond-shaped gap with the absence of the button, a wardrobe faux pas she would not have left the house with.

Her hand flew to the middle of her shirt and clutched at it, as if I was a stranger she'd caught peeping. "Hank, that old Clydesdale, was mad I didn't have any apples and tried to take a chomp out of me for it."

She strode to the kitchen, passing in front of the TV screen.

"Do I get a hello kiss?" I called after her.

"I'm so sweaty," she said without stopping. "I smell like horse crap. Let me have a shower."

She diverted from the kitchen and made for the stairs instead.

"Want company?"

"I just need to get clean."

Her footsteps hammered up the steps and I heard the bathroom door close. A minute later, I heard the spray of the shower hitting the tub. When the water stopped, I heard Eloise moving around in the bathroom for a while, doing whatever it is some women spend so much time doing after a shower. Her footsteps across the ceiling over the kitchen, some fifteen minutes later, told me she'd gone to our bedroom. Ten minutes after that, I heard the creak of our bed as she settled into it.

# 6. Grand Opening

The morning of the grand opening was one filled with tension.

Eloise hadn't spoken anymore about her late night with the horses and I tried my best to give her the benefit of the doubt in my mind. I knew the nightmare I'd had about her and Calvin—a product of my own insecurity—was skewing my judgement and I didn't want to cause our relationship further issues by taking my dreams out on her.

I'd slept on the couch again and had woken up to the sounds of Eloise bustling about in the kitchen; grinding coffee and frying eggs. When I stepped into the kitchen, she was practically dancing around it, putting together a banquet. She looked happier than I'd seen her in the last week.

"What's the occasion?" I asked.

She narrowed her eyes at me and I felt a sliver of ice in my heart. Was I really losing my wife? All over one stupid decision to follow her cousin home? It may have been uncalled for but I had a hard time believing what I'd done could be considered such a heinous offense.

"El," I said, "Can we please talk about all this?"

She flicked the gas off on the stove and slid her eggs onto a plate. "All this what? That you seem to want to sabotage my poor cousin now that he's found something to lay a claim to? Are you jealous my family pursues things they actually enjoy doing instead of settling into whatever bureaucratic purgatory they happened to slide into straight out of college?"

"Eloise."

"Or maybe you don't like him suddenly being the center of attention."

"When did I ever want to be in the spotlight?" I asked. "What's gotten into you?"

"Me?" Her eyebrows shot up. "I'm not the one following people home, trying to ruin them before they've started on their dream."

I didn't know what I was supposed to say. I wanted to shout and throw things but I knew that wasn't going to get me anywhere, not that speaking reasonably was doing much good.

"Okay," I said. "Maybe you'll feel better after the grand opening, once you've seen I haven't sabotaged it."

She only huffed at that.

"I'm going to shower and then I guess we'd better get going. Might get crowded."

She didn't respond so I jogged upstairs before another argument could erupt.

When I came back down twenty minutes later, showered, shaved, and dressed, the house was empty. There was a sticky note on the coffee machine. It said: *Got a ride with Cal. See you there. -E*

I laughed. How was I not supposed to read into that? I had to remind myself she didn't know about my dream, couldn't have any idea where my imagination was taking me. Would she still be acting like this if I'd told her about it?

Part of me didn't want to go anymore, Gobe Bites or no Gobe Bites. I wanted to shrink into myself, find a dark corner deep in my subconscious, and stay there for a long time. I wanted to drive to Jubilee City at top speed and set fire to Nickelsimmer Sweets. I wanted my wife back.

Of course I had no choice about going to the grand opening and, ultimately, even if I thought I could somehow get away with skipping it without making myself look even worse, I couldn't pass up an opportunity to put another one of those delicious morsels in my mouth.

So I would go.

Except things started working against me as soon as I got onto the highway. Minutes after I merged, everything came to a standstill. After fifteen minutes, traffic began to creep forward at the pace of an earthworm in drying cement. I rode it out until the next exit and then diverted, planning on taking the side streets up at least part of the way—I could jump back onto the highway a few miles up, hopefully having skipped the cause of the delay.

The road I chose happened to have a rail crossing inter-secting it and, minutes before I showed up, a sixty-car freight train had stalled out as a result of track vandalism further up the line. This was according to the dweeb who read the traffic on 95.9 The Throb, Jubilee City's home of classic rock—a genre I was horrified to have learned now included music from the 1990's. Traffic piled up behind me, boxing me in. I tried shouting at people in the cars around me to please move so I could get the hell out of here but they either couldn't hear me or pretended not to.

The train took almost an hour to clear out. I tried calling Eloise but her phone went straight to voicemail.

I tried Calvin's and was treated to his voicemail: *"You've reached Calvin Nickelsimmer of Nickelsimmer Sweets. I probably didn't make it to the phone because today is the grand opening of the Nickelsimmer Sweets storefront in Jubilee City. For more information, check out our website at nickelsimmersweets.com. Otherwise, leave a message and I'll get back to you as soon as I'm available."*

I clicked off without leaving a message.

It was three hours past the time the invitation had listed when I pulled into Jubilee City. I spent an additional half an hour looking for parking. By the time I stood in front of the door to Nickelsimmer Sweets, the lights were off inside. I'd missed the whole thing.

Through the display window, I could see confetti and a few crumpled napkins littering the floor. It looked like it had been a real party. I tapped on the glass, not expecting an answer.

Eloise pushed through the door to the back room and stopped short when she saw me standing outside. She arranged her face into a dour, disappointed expression and stalked up to the glass front door. She opened it a crack, as if I was a solicitor she didn't want to make the mistake of acting welcoming toward.

"Nice of you to show up," she said.

"You could have waited for me."

"So you could make sure I didn't get here too?"

I took a deep breath and said, "I'm sorry, El. I'm sorry for all the fighting. I'm sorry I followed your cousin home. I wasn't late on purpose, traffic was working against me."

She shrugged. "What do you want?"

"Can I come in? What's going on? I can help clean up."

"We're having a little afterparty in the back."

"We who?" I shot, unable to keep the edge from my voice.

"My family. Who else?"

Just then, Harrison bumped through the door from the back. He saw me and waved, a surprised smile on his face.

"Look who made it!" he called.

I mustered a smile and gave him a wave.

"Are you going to let me in, El?" I said, searching my wife's face for any sign of affection. My eyes ached and burned and I hoped she could see that whatever was going on was destroying me.

"I think maybe we should just see each other at home," she said. "You upset Calvin a lot when you tailed him. He doesn't exactly feel supported by you."

She may as well have punched me in the stomach. I couldn't catch my breath. It wasn't just not being invited in or the fact that she was mad at me; this was a side of Eloise I'd never seen. As far as I knew, she'd never been cold or callous to anyone for any reason, even those who deserved it. I'd seen her treated like garbage by waitstaff at certain restaurants and still leave a twenty percent tip. She was the most gracious person I knew. It was one of the reasons I'd married her.

"Is there something going on with you two?"

The words were out before I could bite them off, like they'd had a will of their own.

Her face clouded over. "Go home, Arthur."

She pulled the door shut, flicked the deadbolt, and turned her back to me. I watched her shove through the swinging door into the back room. As the door swung open, I caught a glimpse of Calvin with his arm slung over Eloise's father's shoulder. It looked like they were raising a toast.

"You missed some party."

The voice broke through my thoughts, startling me out of them. I looked down in its direction. A thin guy in rumpled, filthy clothes sat propped against the wall of the business next door. He could've been forty-five or sixty-five under his long, gray hair and equally gray beard. I hadn't even noticed him when I approached the shop, even though he stood out against the pristine backdrop of Opal Street.

"Sounded like they was filming a porno in there at one point," the guy said.

I nodded at him, too absorbed in my own hurt to feign interest in what he had to say.

"Caught a whiff of that stuff he was bringing in," he continued, unfazed by my inattentiveness. "Made something stir down there that ain't so much as twitched in a long time." He looked down at his own crotch.

I turned to leave. All I could think about was getting back home so I could get busy pouring hard liquor down my throat.

"He brought in enough cases of them things, he coulda spared me one. Do you have five dollars you could give me so I can get a bowl of soup and a coffee around the corner?"

I spun back to the guy, suddenly cluing in to what he was saying. "You said you watched him load all that stuff in."

The guy licked his lips and nodded. He looked at my pockets as if he expected a fiver to shimmy out of there on its own and leap right into his hand.

"Did you *see* what was in the boxes?" I asked.

He shook his head.

I fished a ten out of my wallet and handed it down to him. "What time was this at?"

My new friend shoved the bill into his pocket then made a show of thinking, sticking his fat, purple tongue out the corner of his mouth and staring up so hard that the whites of his eyes showed. "Musta been around five this morning. Still dark anyhow."

I thanked the guy and headed back to my car. I didn't know why I wanted to know so badly about Calvin's activities. What did I hope to find? The guy was obviously working hard to make his dream happen. Why was I so bent on sabotaging it? Because I was jealous of my wife supporting her cousin?

When I got back home, I mixed myself a scotch and soda then flopped onto the couch and waited for Eloise to get home.

It was after supper when she came through the door holding a small, pink box in one hand. I was on my third drink by then and was feeling pretty good, all things considered. Eloise sat next to me on the couch and placed the box on the table. She stared at me for a long time, neither of us speaking. Then she grasped the lid of the pink box between finger and thumb and lifted it. The aroma was immediate and intense. It set me aflame.

In the box were two bright red squares of pastry. They were topped in what appeared to be powder blue chocolate and had a small, black ball, which looked a lot like a giant fish egg, in the center. Eloise plucked one of the squares from the box and held it up to my mouth. I was powerless to resist, no matter how angry I was. She popped her own into her mouth as I was chewing mine. The flavor was like an eruption of exotic and unidentifiable citrus and berry with a milky undertone that bore the essence along like a magic carpet.

We hadn't even finished chewing when Eloise climbed on top of me. We made love right there for the first time in weeks.

# 7. TALK OF THE TOWN

Things got better between us after that. It was as if all the tension and fighting of the past few weeks had melted away like a spring thaw and underneath was a shining, solid relationship for us to enjoy.

Nickelsimmer Sweets swiftly became the most talked about thing on the internet. People traveled from all over to line up in front of Calvin's shop in hopes of trying one of his legendary treats. Celebrities posted pictures of themselves popping a Nickelsimmer Sweet into their mouths. Social media became flooded by images of the strange and exotic desserts. Message boards speculated about what the ingredients could be. Nobody could keep them out of their mouths for long enough to analyze. The shop sold out of product every day before lunch.

Calvin sold a variety of unusual desserts of seemingly endless flavor combinations and textures though, by far, the most popular were his Gobe Bites, Dream Squares—which Eloise had shared with me on the night of the grand opening—and Angel Nectar, an intensely blue, honey-like substance that, impossibly, always felt warm on the tongue, even after spending hours in the freezer. This last was apparently being used by many as a skin lotion, topical ointment, and personal lubricant.

A sort of black market had developed around Nickelsimmer Sweets, with people reselling the desserts on the street at an insane markup. Even when Calvin instituted a two-items-per-customer policy, stories of people paying upwards of two hundred dollars for a Dream Square flooded the internet. The inevitable fraudsters took advantage of the craze and soon all sorts of whacky desserts were being sold online as the real deal. There were even those who accused Calvin of having stolen the recipes from them but, of course, no one could replicate what he sold in his shop.

The man who had at one time stood awkwardly in the shadows at family gatherings was lauded as the Ambrosia Baron and swiftly became one of the most followed personalities on Instagram. Talk shows and podcasts brought him on to discuss the aphrodisiacal quality of his goods. When asked about it, he would only smile and shrug, telling the interviewer it was never his intention for his desserts to become bedroom aids but that he was glad folks were enjoying them.

Debate swiftly rose around whether or not it was appropriate, or safe, to be giving Nickelsimmer Sweets to children. Calvin would swear up and down they were safe but when asked about the ingredients, he would clam up. He went along with requests to have his desserts sent in for analysis but, unsurprisingly, the treats never seemed to make it to the lab.

It didn't take long for various church organizations, mom groups, and certain influencers to protest out in front of the shop on Opal Street. Nothing, they reasoned, that made people feel so good could be healthy for the body or soul.

Eloise and I picked up a couple of treats every Friday and would lock ourselves in the bedroom until late Saturday morning.

It wasn't that my suspicion of Calvin had eased over those weeks, it was just easier to deal with, especially since things had gotten better with Eloise and I. But I still had to wonder if our marriage would be as good as it was without Nickelsimmer Sweets. What would happen if I just didn't pick them up one weekend? I wish now I'd tested that theory, or, for that matter, that I'd never heard of Calvin "the Ambrosia Baron" Nickelsimmer.

It was the middle of summer, ten weeks after the grand opening, that I got the call from Rick, my supervisor.

"Nickelsimmer Sweets," he said, as if that should tell me everything I needed to know.

I'd been driving between inspections, cruising along the highway and enjoying the sun on my face. I smiled into the windshield as though Rick had been watching me through it.

"They're something alright," I said.

"You requested the follow up inspection."

It wasn't a question so I didn't answer. I'd completely forgotten about the follow up visit by then. I'd been wrapped up in Nickelsimmer fever with the rest of the world.

"Now I see why, you sneaky devil," Rick said.

Shit. Busted. He'd found out I was Calvin's cousin, if only by marriage, and now I'd be facing some sort of disciplinary action for the conflict of interest.

"You're just looking for an excuse to stock up on goodies, aren't you? Hoping for a little bribe?"

I remained silent. I felt my face flushing. Whether he thought I was accepting bribes or doing favors for my family, both meant trouble for me.

Rick laughed, a deep, boisterous guffaw that blasted through my car speakers. "Just messing around with you, Duk. Relax for goodness sake. Look, with all the hubbub around these things, we need to get this inspection done quick or someone's gonna catch wind he's operating under a provisional certificate. I don't know about you but those desserts of his have vastly improved my marriage and I don't want them going away anytime soon, you get me?"

I found my voice and said that, yes, I did get him.

"Make it tomorrow," Rick said. "I'll clear your schedule for the first half of the day. Get there early so as few people see you as possible. You know what some idiots start thinking just seeing us in a place."

It was true. There was often at least one patron who, upon seeing my badge, would stop me in a restaurant to ask if I was there for some big health violation. People love to imagine the worst, which I suppose is something I can relate to.

I told Rick that I'd be there first thing tomorrow—I happened to know when the owner got to work in the morning.

# 8. FOLLOW UP

I had to leave my house at an ungodly hour to make it to the shop before Calvin arrived. I hadn't called ahead to warn him about the inspection. I tried to tell myself it wasn't because I wanted to trap him, but I couldn't shake the feeling that I would catch him in the act of something. I was reasonably certain he still wasn't making the desserts on site, which meant I would have to see the production area, wherever that happened to be. Deep in my subconscious, I knew I was motivated by my own curiosity more than any desire to ensure his operation was on the level. I *needed* to see how Nickelsimmer Sweets were made, where the magic came from.

The sky was an orange-gold ahead of the sunrise as I pulled into my usual parking spot around the corner from the shop. I took a moment to finish the last cold dregs of my coffee, slung my bag over my shoulder, and hoofed it to the storefront.

Minutes after I arrived, Calvin pulled up in his Mercedes, once silver and now wrapped in pink vinyl that looked garish in the morning light. The company logo, with nickelsimmersweets.com written underneath it, was plastered on every angle of the car, just as he'd described it to me the first time I'd made a surprise visit to his shop. Calvin looked shocked when he spotted me through the windshield but a smile quickly appeared on his face.

"What's up, cuz?" he called to me as he climbed out of the car.

I patted my shoulder bag. "Inspection time, I'm afraid. Boss called me last minute. Sorry I couldn't give you a heads up." The lie slid out easily.

"Don't suppose you can just give me my certificate and have done with it?"

I shook my head. "We'll both regret it if I'm caught doing that."

He was quiet for a long moment, one hand tapping the roof of his car.

After an uncomfortably long silence, he popped his trunk and said, "Okay, help me load in these boxes and we'll get to it."

Pink boxes, similar to the one he'd brought to Christmas, now bearing the company logo, were tightly packed into the trunk of the car. More were stacked in the back and in the passenger seat. I lost count but there must have been at least two dozen of them. The aroma from within wafted out and into my nostrils, almost physically pulling me toward the boxes. I was reminded of the old cartoons in which a tantalizing odor would be depicted as a vaporous hand, beckoning with one finger for some hapless anthropomorphic animal to give in to temptation and fall into whatever trap had been set by the cruel protagonist—pies loaded with dynamite more often than not, the lit fuse apparently rendered invisible to the victim by the assault on their olfactory glands.

We loaded the boxes into the shop and it took every ounce of my willpower not to peak inside them. We brought them to the pristine back room—that still hadn't been equipped with anything more than stainless-steel counters—and loaded them into the otherwise empty walk-in fridge.

When we loaded the last of the boxes in, Calvin spread his arms and gestured around the space. "Well? Pass?"

I wished then that I hadn't requested to do the follow-up visit, that I'd stuck to my guns and let another inspector handle it so that I didn't have to put family on the spot like this. The irony was that I'd finally caved and asked to be assigned the second inspection because I'd wanted to mend the rift that I'd inadvertently dug between Calvin and myself. It had also been a show of good faith to Eloise that I supported her cousin. I was tired of all the melodrama over a dessert.

"Are these boxes full of finished product?" I asked.

Calvin only looked at me.

I said, "You know I have to see the production area, right? I can't issue the certificate without it."

A hard-to-define emotion moved across Calvin's face. He looked angry and amused and impatient all at once. He also appeared to be thinking hard about something. Considering. Weighing consequences.

"Don't suppose it can wait until the end of the business day?" he said, voice flat.

"Sorry."

He let out a long breath through his nose. "I think you probably know I make this stuff at home."

I nodded.

He slammed a palm on the counter but still managed to treat me to that confident Nickelsimmer smile he'd perfected throughout his success.

"I'll drive, I guess," he said.

"I'll follow you."

The trip back to his place was easy since we were moving against the morning traffic coming into the city. Calvin sped the whole way, unnecessarily weaving between lanes as he passed more leisurely drivers. I kept to just over the speed limit but he didn't let me get left behind. He would slow down enough for me to catch up before darting ahead again until he was almost out of site.

The sun was fully risen, already heating up the day considerably by the time we pulled into the long driveway in front of Calvin's house. I remembered my nightmare, the one in which I'd walked in on him and Eloise. The house stared down at me in reality the same way it had in my dream. Even against a perfectly blue summer sky, it made me uneasy to look at.

Calvin strode up the driveway without a word to me. He jogged up the steps, unlocked the door, and held it open, naked impatience on his face.

"You're absolutely sure this is necessary?" he asked as I approached.

"Wish I could say otherwise. I'll try to make it quick."

For a brief moment, he looked sad, like he was resigned to having to do something he didn't want to do. I didn't read into it—my only concern was that I might potentially uncover some practices that would need to be corrected; proper dishwashing, food storage, that sort of thing.

Calvin gestured through the door and I stepped inside.

I was unprepared for the smell. That is, I was prepared for there to be a smell, some sort of aroma that would give this place away as a house in which things are baked, but it smelled like any normal home. A bit musty, maybe.

It was dark inside, the only light coming through narrow parts in the heavy floor-to-ceiling drapes that covered the huge windows. Through the gloom, I could see the kitchen straight ahead, at the rear of the house. I started in that direction but Calvin stopped me.

"Over here," he said, holding open another door. "Production's in the basement."

That explained why it didn't smell like a bakery on the main level, though I would've expected some of the smell to bleed upstairs. I figured the scent of the house's age was masking the more pleasing aromas of confection.

Calvin led the way into the basement, which was almost completely dark. He ignored me when I asked about turning on a light. I sniffed at the air but all I could smell was more mustiness and something much less pleasant underneath; almost like rot. It was what I imagined an old grave must smell like.

My host waited for me at the bottom of the stairs, standing in front of a huge plastic sheet that covered off the rest of the basement. Once more I was reassured that here was another layer to keep the bakery smells contained. Was he paranoid of anyone finding out he made his stuff here? It wasn't as though he had any neighbors to speak of.

I reached the bottom of the stairs and noticed the floor

was hard-packed earth. Already that was something that would need to be addressed, unless he'd put flooring down in his production area.

"Last chance," Calvin said. "You sure you want to spoil the magic?"

In the gloom of the basement, Calvin's eyes were dark and expressionless. I was reminded of a spider crawling across its web toward a juicy insect that had been foolish or inattentive enough to become ensnared by it. A faint alarm went off in the primal part of my brain; a survival instinct that had been squashed down by generations of relatively easy, threat-free living. I recognized it for what it was but I'd lived my entire life without facing real danger. I dismissed the feeling as I would if I'd been watching a scary movie, assuring myself there couldn't possibly be a threat here. Calvin was family.

"Let's just get this done so you can get back to work," I said.

He looked away from me then, but not before I spotted a knowing grin spread across his face. He pulled back the plastic sheet and held it for me.

"Step inside, then," he said.

I ducked through the plastic and was immediately struck by the smell, which was so far from what I'd expected that I actually gagged. Instead of the sweet smell of sugar and the warm aroma of butter, the grave-like stench intensified, only now it smelled like a carrion pit that had been open to the sun for a week.

I could barely see the ground I walked on and waited just inside the plastic for Calvin to lead the way.

"What is this, Cal?"

"Ssh," he said from behind me. "You'll see. Look just there and let your eyes adjust."

He grabbed me by the chin and oriented my face so I was looking in the right direction.

At first there was still only the dark. I was about to ask if he was playing a prank on me when I spotted it; a dull, orange glow coming from the floor twenty feet or so ahead of me. My first thought was that it was a sub-basement but I could see no opening into it, just that glowing spot on the floor, almost like the earth itself was the source of the light.

Calvin took me by the hand and pulled me forward. It felt like an oddly intimate gesture.

We crossed the earthen floor to where the glow emanated. It grew brighter the closer we got to it, almost as if it anticipated our presence.

When we came within a few feet of it, the earth in the middle of the orange light opened up like a mouth. I leapt back from it and screamed in surprise and horror. Calvin quickly wrapped a hand over my mouth to silence me.

"Don't startle her," he whispered.

I barely registered what he said. I gaped at the new hole in the floor, big enough to drive a car through, orange light spilling out of it. The luminescence came from the glistening walls of the orifice, like they were soaked in glowstick fluid. The tunnel led down in a gentle slope and seemed to go on forever. A warm, fetid air wafted out of it and forced its way into my nostrils. As a kid I'd had a dog that loved to eat dead things it found outside. Once, I watched him eat the rotting, maggot-ridden carcass of a squirrel he found in our backyard. An hour later, he'd puked the thing back up all over my bed. The tunnel smelled like that regurgitated mess; like death and rot and stomach juices. I pulled my shirt up over my nose.

"What the hell is this?" I asked again.

Calvin only walked ahead of me, into the tunnel. He didn't look back to see if I would follow. Not wanting to be left alone, and spurred by an insane curiosity, I jogged to keep up.

The floor of the tunnel was soft under my shoes and gleamed with that orange phosphorescence. The stench seeped through my shirt and into my nose. Breathing through my mouth was no help; I could taste the air, which felt tantamount to licking up the gore my old dog had spewed onto my bed.

We walked for a very long time. I asked Calvin what we were doing in here, how far the tunnel could possibly go, what this had to with his desserts, but each of my inquiries were met with silence. All I could do was follow.

After we'd walked for what might have been half a mile, the tunnel opened up into a cavernous space too big to see the walls of. Calvin stopped and stood in the middle of the cave with his hands on his hips. Something moved in the shadows just beyond him.

"You're not going to tell me you make your desserts down here, are you?" I asked him.

He looked at me and grinned. "You still think I make them? Are you that willfully ignorant?"

I was. Because I didn't want to think about the implications being presented to me.

"My dad bought this house for him and my mom to retire in," Calvin said, looking up into the darkness above.

Something dripped off to my left.

"He dug this cave?" I said.

Calvin ignored me. "My mom hated it. Didn't want to have to fix up a place to retire in. Her idea of retirement was the exact opposite. She wanted to move to Florida and live in a nice condo for the rest of their lives. Dad tried to make her see the potential of this place. Then they found this," he spread his arms wide, "And my mom wanted him to burn the place to the ground. Can you imagine? Finding something truly wondrous and wanting to set fire to it? Dad tried to talk her out of it but she came down here with a can of gas and a box of matches anyway. He found the empty canister just back there," Calvin pointed back to the tunnel we'd come through. "Never saw her again after that.

"Soon after, Dad discovered what I've turned into my livelihood. Only he had no foresight. He worked in a factory his whole life, there wasn't an ounce of business sense in him. He hoarded it all. Can you imagine him, stuffing his face with those things and no one to love but himself? When I came back from school, I found him down here, laying on the ground, naked, just going to town on himself," Calvin made the universal jerking off gesture. "I dragged him out and got him to tell me about what he'd discovered. I tried to talk him into marketing it but he became furious with me. Told me I was trying to rob him, to take away what was rightfully his. Then he kicked me out and told me he didn't want to see me again."

I wanted to be sympathetic, to try to commiserate with the poor guy. But there were pressing questions to be answered, questions I wasn't sure I wanted the answer to but that I desperately needed to ask.

"Calvin, where do your desserts come from?"

He raised a finger to silence me. Or to tell me he'd get to it. Or both.

"I only saw Dad twice more before he died," Calvin said. "The first time, I was stupid enough to think he might have come around, that I could convince him I wasn't trying to steal from him at least. He chased me off as soon as I pulled in the driveway."

I didn't bother reminding Calvin he'd done the same thing to me the first time I'd come here.

He went on, "The next time was about a week before he died. Dad actually called me. Told me we needed to talk. That was when I met them. Dad thought he'd offer me to them. But I knew they wanted what *she* wanted. The whole point is to spread her seed, to bring her to the world she wasn't made to exist in by changing it to be more like her. How can that possibly be achieved if you're hoarding what was meant to be given away?" His voice grew increasingly manic the more he spoke.

"Where do the desserts come from?" I asked again, though any notion of a health inspection was far gone from my mind.

Calvin looked at me with eyes like the depths of the ocean; a liquid void. Had they grown darker, bigger since we got here? Movement behind him caught my eye as something resembling legs scurried deeper into the shadows.

"We sow her seed and that's so important," Calvin said. "We take her from her prison and spread her farther than her form could ever hope to travel. We do so willingly. And for that, she makes it the most pleasurable thing we could hope to experience.

"That's what Dad didn't understand. That's why they

took him away when the metamorphosis came over him. He brought me down here to give to her, but my servitude to her purpose is more valuable than any nutrients I could hope to offer her from my body."

Forms emerged from the shadows behind him. Insectile and utterly alien, they inched forward, as though growing more confident that I didn't pose a threat to them, that I could be overtaken. They stood upright on two or four limbs, it was hard to tell which in the dim, orange light and by the way they constantly scurried and twitched. Their chitinous upper limbs—like arms—gripped gleaming tools that screamed violent intentions. A papery web of flesh hung between their arms and bodies. They crowded behind Calvin, dozens of them, analyzing me, assessing me with darting glances and invertebrate twists of the neck.

Off to the side of the cavern, one of these things scurried over to a protuberance growing up out of the floor. It was glistening and orange, like the walls, and grew up in a thin stalk that ended in a round bulb the size of a bowling ball. The creature raised its tool—a scythe-like thing made of what looked like the same chitin that covered the creatures' bodies—over the bulb and hacked at it, ripping through it with some effort. A deep green ooze sprayed from the bulb as the thing slashed at it. Once the creature had torn a hole the size of my hand in the bulb, it shoved the tool in and dug it around inside. For an insane second, it looked like it was scooping the guts out of a pumpkin. As it scraped in the growth, a deep, pain-filled screech that vibrated my teeth echoed through the cavern. The screech grew louder when the creature pulled its tool, covered in viscous, green gore, from the bulb. Something was stuck to the tip of the tool. The creature ripped it from the blade and shook the green gunk from it. When I recognized what the thing held, I leaned over and retched.

It was a Gobe Bite. I could smell it even from where I stood, a dozen feet away, alluring in spite of my disgust.

The creature brought the thing to Calvin, who accepted it as if from a slave.

"Incredible, isn't it?" he said, taking a chomp out of the Gobe Bite like it was an apple. "Oh my God, it never gets old. She just gives this stuff to us!"

"You keep saying 'she'. Who is she?" I said.

He raised his arms over his head and turned in a circle. "She's all around us."

"We're inside her?"

"In what we might call her ovaries if our concept of biology could come close to understanding what she is."

"I don't understand," I said, backing away from him. "You climbed into this thing and just started eating the crap you found in it?"

Calvin gestured to the growing crowd of bug-things. "They offered it to me. I think they're like remora; those fish that latch onto whales. They serve her body and, in turn, are housed and fed by her."

He tossed the Gobe Bite behind him and the creatures fell upon it, clawing at each other to get to it. The melee was over in seconds and, when the crowd dispersed, two of them were left laying on the ground, motionless and missing several limbs. Orange tendrils grew out of the floor and over top of the carcasses like weeds. In seconds, they were just another bump in the floor, being digested for all I knew.

"Perfect eco-system," Calvin said, looking up from where the creatures had been buried. "And soon enough, it will be up there."

He pointed above him and when he did, his t-shirt pulled back a bit, exposing the underside of his arm.

"You have something stuck to you," I said.

It was just something to say. Words to help me deal with my shock.

Calvin looked down at his arm and his eyes, which had definitely grown bigger, widened. They were the same eyes as the bug-things, I realized. And the stuff under his arm, which he was tugging at now, was the same webbing those things had beneath their own limbs. Calvin had used the word metamorphosis earlier and I'd let the term slip by me, never dreaming he was speaking of something literal.

"No, no, no," he muttered. "Not yet. Mine is to be last. A grand transformation! I'm to be her king!"

He was shouting at the creatures, which were closing in on him now.

He turned to me and begged me with his eyes as insect limbs wrapped around his arms and torso, pulling him back into the shadows with them.

"Arthur, get me out of here," he said. "Please. I'll make you a lieutenant. These things are confused—they serve *me*!"

The cavern rumbled and a moan came from far in its depths, a sound that conveyed what I thought sounded like a weary annoyance. I tried not to imagine where it originated from, what the whole picture of this thing I stood within might look like. It had to be colossal. How far must it stretch underground? Was there only one tunnel to the surface? A singular exposed orifice?

Instead of dwelling on it, I ran.

Calvin's screams followed my flight but by the time I emerged into his basement, the cries had been silent for at least a minute.

The walls of the tunnel grew brighter as I tumbled out of it, onto the dirt floor of the basement. Would those things follow me out? I scrambled back from the opening, screaming when I bumped into the plastic sheet. I couldn't tear my eyes from the pulsing orange light coming from the hole in front of me. I expected to see a clawed appendage reach out from its depths at any second. Instead, the hole closed in on itself until it was little more than a fleshy, puckered anus in the floor.

I stumbled up the stairs, hyperventilating, mind racing to decide what to do next. I spilled out the back door, into Calvin's overgrown yard. I imagined the thing I'd been standing inside stretching out underground as far as my eye could see.

My gaze landed on his garden shed and I knew what I had to do next.

# 9. FINAL AUDIT

Setting the house on fire had been easier than I'd expected it to be. I had thought I'd meet resistance, either from the remora bugs or the thing Calvin had only referred to as *her*. Nothing came out of the hole to meet me though, even as I doused it in gasoline from one of the two canisters I'd found in the shed. I'd emptied all of one into the basement and soaked as much of the main floor as I could with the second.

I watched the place burn for as long as I thought I could get away with. The house was isolated but someone was bound to see the smoke and call the fire department eventually. Or not, I didn't care which. I took off when the upper level collapsed on the rest of the house, turning it into a burning pit. Then I drove home.

On the drive back to my house, I thought about the lack of opposition to my assault of fire. Had the thing under the house burned up with it or was it more resilient than that? Or, worse, had it managed to flee the scene, burrowing deeper underground?

Eloise wasn't home when I got back so I had time to shower and firm up an alibi, which it turned out I hadn't even needed. I told my superiors I'd waited for hours but that Calvin hadn't shown up to his shop that morning. When it was discovered that there was no equipment in his shop and that he'd likely been making his desserts at home, the assumption was that he'd burned the place down accidentally while baking. I was sure the fire marshal would discover gasoline was used to start the fire but apparently they hadn't felt the need to look into it any further. Lucky me.

The big news, of course, was that it looked like Nickelsimmer Sweets was no more. Nobody mentioned the boxes of those things he and I had unloaded into his shop. Likely the landlord of the place had discovered them and kept them to himself. I wish I'd thought of getting there first and maybe burning the shop down as well, for good measure. Not that it would have done much good in the grand scheme of things.

For a short time, I patted myself on the back for a job well done, even if it was considered a national tragedy that Nickelsimmer Sweets had met its end. I really thought I'd taken care of things. Saved the world.

But reports of a strange illness have started cropping up. People undergoing drastic physiological changes, including the growth of new limbs and the hardening of skin. Some people seemed to lose their minds as a result of the mysterious sickness and have been caught trying to burrow into the earth. An online video I watched showed one such person, a young guy of twenty or so, clawing at the earth with hands that were raw and bloody. A woman I assumed was his mother tried to pull him away from the hole he was digging but he threw her off, screaming, "*I have to get to her!*" He had the same big, black eyes Calvin had right before the remora bugs took him.

This morning, I watched Eloise towel off after getting out of the shower. Under her arm, like webbing, was stretched a thin, papery membrane. She caught me staring and at first smiled at me before a shadow of concern came over her face.

"Arthur," she said, stepping closer to me. "What's wrong with your eyes?"

I had to confess everything then. It's not fair that she should suffer through this in ignorance. She's crying on our bed. There's a faint buzzing to her voice that wasn't there last night.

I'm staring in the mirror now, getting used to my eyes. They've grown and darkened so that they resemble the arachnid eyes I'd seen on Calvin's face. The urge to dig has flitted through my mind, almost like a hunger pang. I'm not worried though; I won't be digging random holes in our back yard.

I know exactly where to find her.

# GRATITUDE

Big thanks goes out to M Willis Wardle for his support, for being one of the first to read this gross little story, and not least of all for creating the sexy cover design. M is the author of a kids/YA horror called The Chilling Adventures of the Monster Kids and puts out an old-timey radio show-style podcast called Zip Zapperdoodle, which I highly recommend. Thanks for the support, man.

# About the Author

Christopher Sweet is the author of the horror/magical-realism novel *The Boy in the Canvas*. He's also penned several dozen short stories and multiple screenplays.

He's worked as a freelance writer, manager, waiter, bartender, event DJ, actor, children's entertainer, truck driver, shopkeeper, call center operator, concierge, office assistant, barista, and currently works as a campground manager. He loves books, movies, the outdoors, and baseball.

He lives with his growing tribe of humans and beasts in New Brunswick, Canada.

You can catch him online at:
www.authorchristophersweet.com

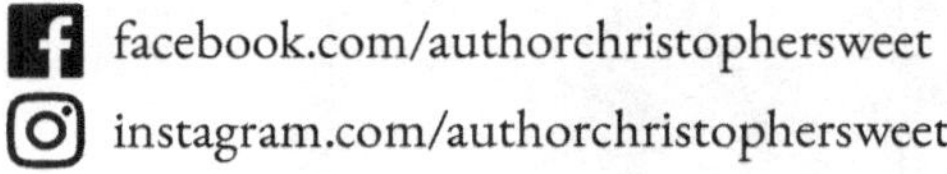

facebook.com/authorchristophersweet

instagram.com/authorchristophersweet

www.ingramcontent.com/pod-product-compliance
Lightning Source LLC
Chambersburg PA
CBHW021749190726
48290CB00008B/2545